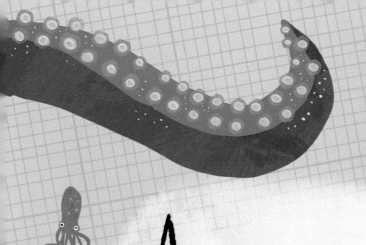

Amazing Mums

Facts and stories about all kinds of awesome mums

by Gabrielle Kuzak

illustrated by Hannah Broadway

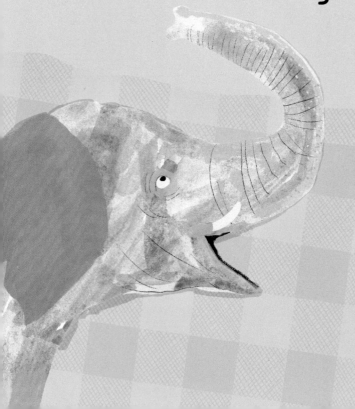

First published in the UK in 2021 by Peahen Publishing Ltd
www.peahenpublishing.com

Text copyright © 2021 Gabrielle Kuzak
Illustration copyright © 2021 Hannah Broadway

ISBN: 978-1-8381099-3-6

A CIP catalogue record for this is available
from the British Library

Paper sourced from sustainable forests

A donation to The Treesisters will be made
with every purchase of this book

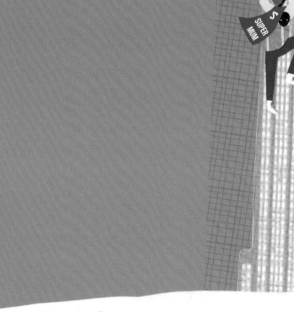

SUPER MUM

Peahen
Publishing

To Harry, Jacob and Joshua.
You know I'd fight a bear to protect you!
Love, your mum x.
GK

To Little Bear & Mr Pips
I love you.
HB

"My mum's amazing!

After I was born, I clung to her tummy and she carried me everywhere – even when she was foraging for food, swinging from trees or running through the jungle.

My mum carries me the WHOLE TIME, keeping me safe.

My mum is a super
nest-builder...she spends
a lot of her time up in the
trees where she builds a new
nest every single night.

She pulls together large branches
and weaves together smaller
branches to make me a mattress,
and if it's raining, she makes a roof
out of big leaves to keep me dry."

Did you know an
orangutan mother can
make up to 15,000
nests for her young
in her lifetime?

"My mum's amazing!

Mum built a large nest out of mud, sticks and plants to keep me and my brothers and sisters warm in our eggs.

She stayed close by to protect us from predators, like large birds and lizards.

After we'd hatched, she carefully placed us in her **enormous** jaws, leaving them open slightly so we were safe from her large, sharp teeth and carried us to the water."

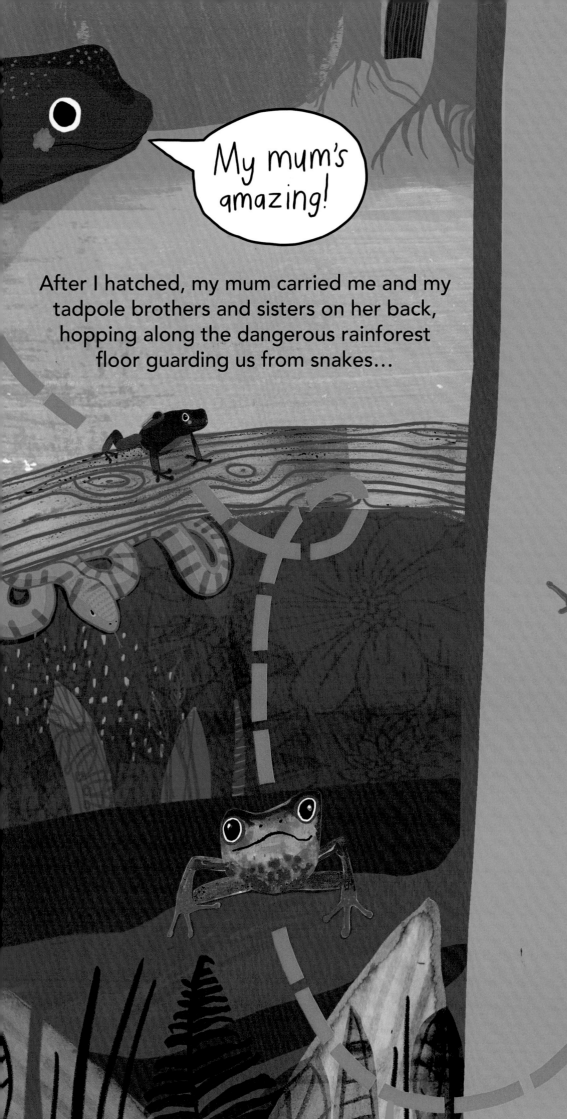

My mum's amazing!

After I hatched, my mum carried me and my tadpole brothers and sisters on her back, hopping along the dangerous rainforest floor guarding us from snakes…

before climbing up to

30

metres –

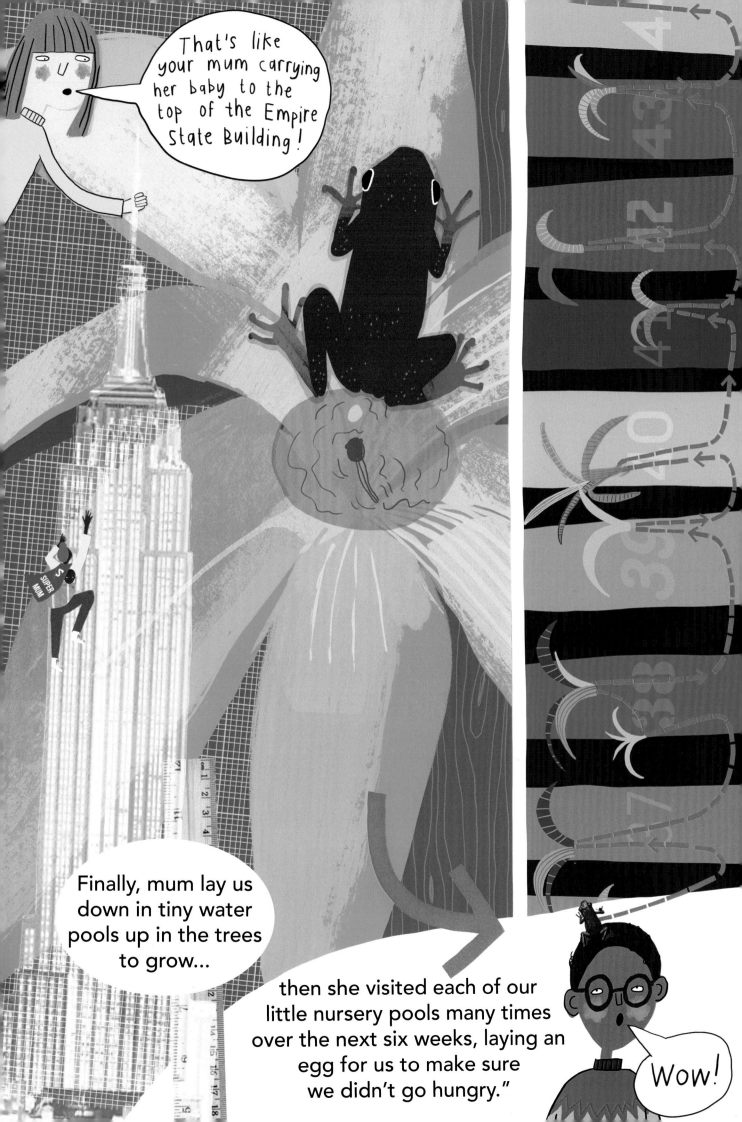

"My mum's amazing!

When I was born, I made my way to a special fur-lined pouch my mum has at the front of her tummy. Mum's pouch protected me, keeping me warm and cosy, and giving me milk.

My mum can have a few babies in her pouch at the same time. She can have a newborn (called a pinkie) and a **bigger** baby (called a joey) together!

I stayed in her pouch for nine months, then it was time for me to hop out. Even though I'm **bigger**, if I get scared, I can do a forward **somersault** into her pouch. It's a bit of a squash!"

The herd is made up of all the females in my family: my mum, my aunts, cousins and my grandmothers with my brother and sisters. All the elephants help to look after me.

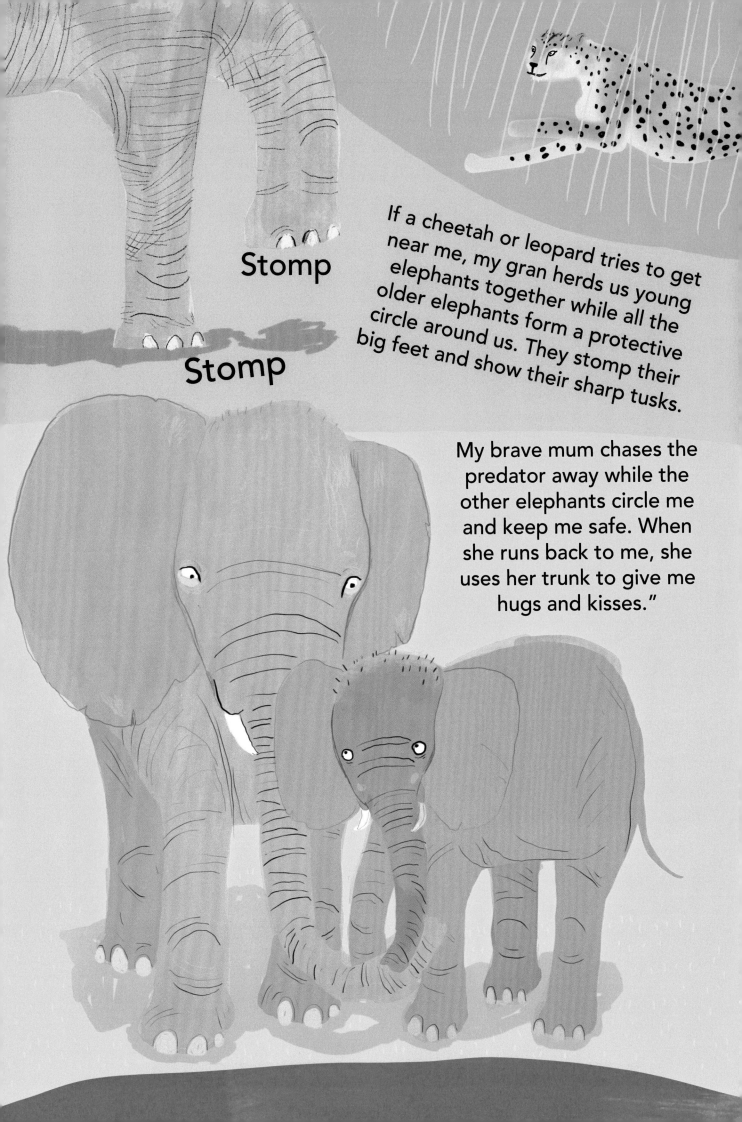

Stomp

Stomp

If a cheetah or leopard tries to get near me, my gran herds us young elephants together while all the older elephants form a protective circle around us. They stomp their big feet and show their sharp tusks.

My brave mum chases the predator away while the other elephants circle me and keep me safe. When she runs back to me, she uses her trunk to give me hugs and kisses."

"My mum's amazing!

When I was born, my mum kept me safely hidden in a den, where she stayed with me for eight weeks. Then I was introduced to the rest of my family, which is called a pride. The pride is made up of my aunts, sisters, cousins and grandmothers who are all called lionesses, with a couple of male lions who defend the family.

Did you know that a lion cub's mum is one of the fastest runners in the world? She can run up to 50 miles per hour!

My mum does most of the hunting and starts teaching me to hunt when I'm about three months old.

My mum is really brave and would do anything to protect me. If predators like hyenas and leopards, or other angry male lions get too close to me, she roars and snarls and chases them away."

She **never** leaves us, not even to eat when she's hungry, and she does this for many months, even years.

She defends us from large fish and whales,

and keeps us safe and clean by blowing bubbles over us and cleaning us with her suckers.

Once we hatch, Mum carefully pushes all my brothers, sisters and me out to sea, so we can find our own homes."

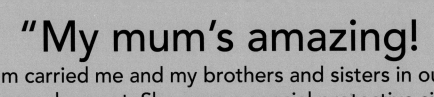

"My mum's amazing!

My mum carried me and my brothers and sisters in our eggs wherever she went. She spun a special protective silk sac around us, like a tiny round silken globe and attached the sac to her, where we stayed until we hatched.

Mum has to move much more slowly carrying us all and has to keep stopping when one of us falls off!

She does this for days, until we climb off and go and hunt on our own."

Bye Mum!

"My mum's amazing!

My mum built a snow den in the banks of a snowdrift, so we had a safe place to be born, protecting us from the freezing cold and predators, like arctic foxes.

Polar bear mums usually give birth to twins and once we're born, we cuddle in close to Mum and she feeds us very nutritious milk which helps us grow quickly.

We stay in the den for four to six months before we venture outside. Mum hasn't eaten in all that time so is very hungry!

If a predator turns up, like a fox or a cat, she quickly rounds us up and herds us to safety.

She spreads her wings out as wide as possible and curves them, then charges at the attacker, cackling fiercely and pecking at them.

Then she gathers us close under her wings and clucks affectionately, letting us know we are safe."

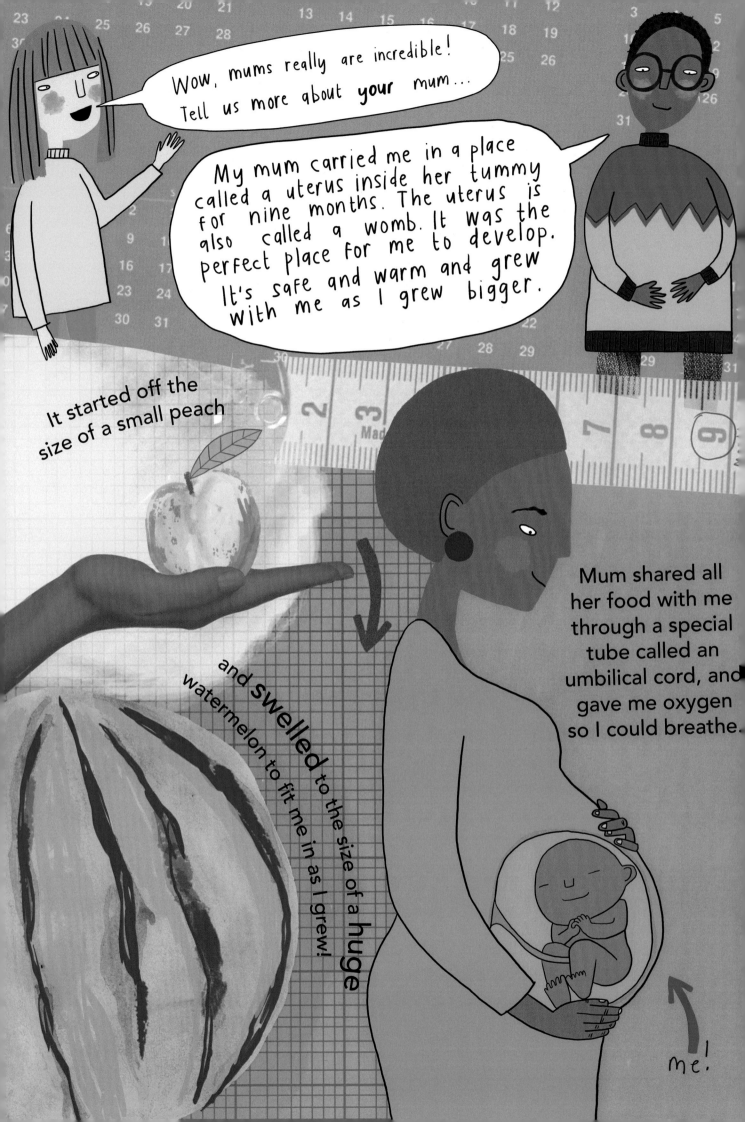

HEAVYWEIGHT CHAMPION MUM

TOP CLIMBER MUM

M U M

BEST SINGLE MUM

GREAT MUM ON NO SLEEP

Thank you for being my mummy!

ULTIMATE PROTECTOR MUM

BEST TEAM PLAYER MUMMY

Dolphin

Dolphins can be found in a wide range of the world's oceans, seas and rivers.

Polar bear

Wolf Spider

Strawberry Poison Dart Frog

They live just about anywhere! While some species are found on cold rocky mountain tops, others live in volcanic lava tubes. From deserts to rainforests, grasslands to suburban lawns, wolf spiders thrive; there's likely one nearby.

North Polar Region

Queen Elizabeth Islands

Greenland

Svalbard

Russia

Alaska

Hudson Bay

America

Asia

Africa

Borneo

Central & South America

Sumatra

Austr

Elephant

Crocodile

Orangutan

Octopuses are found in every ocean in the world.

Chickens live everywhere now, but originally came from the tropical jungles of Southeast Asia.

Lion

Kangaroo

Octopus

Chicken